For Sebastian
K.H.

For Alexander, Jessica and Joel
J.E.

Text copyright © 1992 by Kathy Henderson
Illustrations copyright © 1992 by Jennifer Eachus
All rights reserved. No part of this book may be reproduced or
transmitted in any form or by any means, electronic or
mechanical, including photocopying, recording, or by any
information storage and retrieval system, without permission in
writing from the Publisher.

Macmillan Publishing Company is part of the
Maxwell Communication Group of Companies.

Macmillan Publishing Company
866 Third Avenue
New York, NY 10022

Originally published by Walker Books Ltd., London, England.

First American edition. Printed in Hong Kong.

1 3 5 7 9 10 8 6 4 2

Library of Congress Cataloging-in-Publication Data
Henderson, Kathy.
In the middle of the night / written by Kathy Henderson ;
illustrated by Jennifer Eachus. — 1st American ed.
p.   cm.
Summary: During the night while almost everyone is asleep,
cleaners, bakers, astronomers, nurses, doctors, and many others
carry on with their work.
ISBN 0-02-743545-8
[1. Night—Fiction.   2. City and town life—Fiction.]
I. Eachus, Jennifer, ill.   II. Title.
PZ7.H3805In   1992   [E]—dc20   91-29982

IN THE MIDDLE OF THE NIGHT

Written by Kathy Henderson
Illustrated by Jennifer Eachus

MACMILLAN PUBLISHING COMPANY
NEW YORK

MAXWELL MACMILLAN INTERNATIONAL   NEW YORK OXFORD SINGAPORE SYDNEY

A long time after bedtime
when it's very very late
when even dogs dream
and there's deep sleep
breathing through the house

when the doors are locked
and the curtains drawn
and the shops are dark
and the last train's gone
and there's no more traffic in the street
because everyone's asleep

then

the window cleaner comes
to the main street shop fronts
and polishes the glass
in the street-lit dark

and a big truck rumbles past
on its way to the dump
loaded with the last
of the old day's trash.

On the twentieth floor
of the office tower
there's a lighted window
and high up there
another night cleaner's
vacuuming the floor
working nights on her own
while her children sleep at home.

And down in the dome of the observatory
the astronomer who's waited all day for the dark
is watching the good black sky at last
for stars and moons
and spikes of light
through her telescope
in the middle of the night
while everybody sleeps.

At the bakery
the bakers in their floury clothes
mix dough in machines
for tomorrow's loaves of bread

and out by the gate
rows of parked vans wait
for their drivers to come
and take the newly baked
bread to the shops
for the time when the
bread eaters wake.

Across the town at the hospital
where the nurses watch in the dim-lit wards
someone very old shuts their eyes
and dies
breathes their very last breath
on their very last night.

Yet not far away on another floor
after months of waiting
a new baby's born
and the mother and the father
hold the baby and smile
and the baby looks up
and the world's just begun

but still everybody sleeps.

Now through the silent station
past the empty shops
and the office towers
past the sleeping streets
and the hospital
a train with no windows
goes rattling by

and inside the train the sorters sift
urgent letters and packets on the late night shift
so tomorrow's mail will arrive in time
at the towns and the villages down the line.

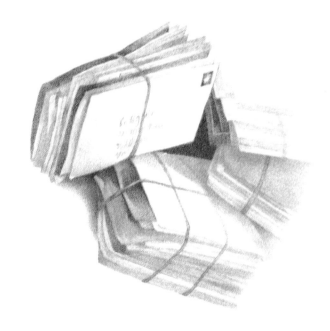

And the mother
with the wakeful child in her arms
walking up and down
and up and down
and up and down
the room
hears the train as it passes by
and the cats in the yard
and the night owl's flight
and hums hushabye and hushabye
we should be asleep now
you and I
it's late and time to close your eyes

it's the middle of the night.